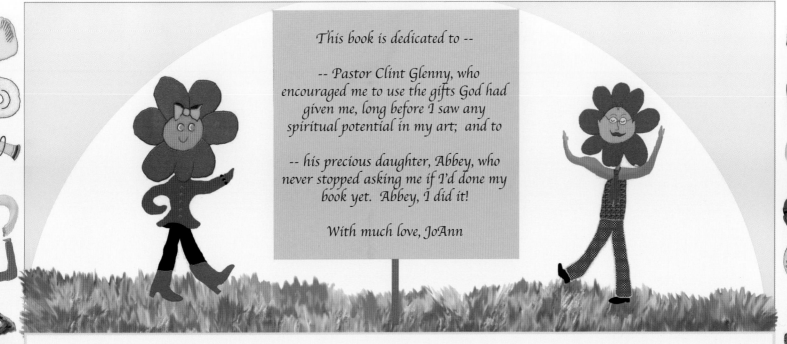

This book is dedicated to --

-- Pastor Clint Glenny, who encouraged me to use the gifts God had given me, long before I saw any spiritual potential in my art; and to

-- his precious daughter, Abbey, who never stopped asking me if I'd done my book yet. Abbey, I did it!

With much love, JoAnn

Printed in Hong Kong

Illustrations were created by JoAnn DeJoria Smith

copyright © 1974, 1993 & 2001 by JoAnn DeJoria Smith

Scriptures adapted from King James Version of The Holy Bible
by Stan & JoAnn DeJoria Smith

ISBN Number 0-9715405-0-0

Published by:
Sonrose Publishers

Sold and Licensed to the trade by:
Global Publishing Services
6487 NW Lamonta Road
Prineville, Oregon 97754-8230

1974, 1993 & 2001
by JoAnn DeJoria Smith

The Alphabuddies™

JESUS LOVES YOU

This Book Belongs To:

_____

A Gift From:_____

Date:_____

Occasion:_____

A Special Prayer For You:_____

_____

_____

_____

_____

ALPHABUDDIES

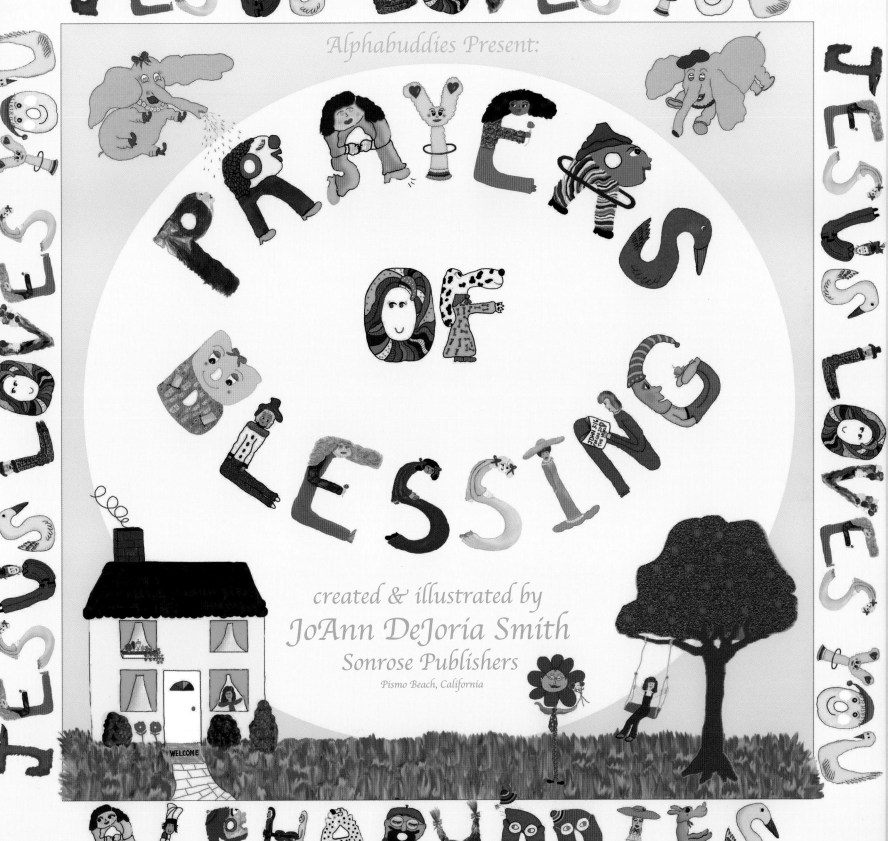

Alphabuddies Present:

PRAYERS OF BLESSING

created & illustrated by
JoAnn DeJoria Smith
Sonrose Publishers
Pismo Beach, California

JESUS LOVES YOU

WELCOME

ALPHABUDDIES

AND ENLARGE MY LAND.

BLESSINGS

BLESSINGS

1 Chronicles 4:10

THE JABEZ PRAYER

GOD'S PRESENCE

GOD'S PRESENCE

MAY YOU ALWAYS BE WITH ME

1 Chronicles 4:10

THE JABEZ PRAYER

1 Chronicles 4:10

PRAYER OF MOSES

MAY THE LORD BLESS YOU AND KEEP YOU

Numbers 6:24

PROTECTION

PRAYER OF MOSES

MAY HE SMILE ON YOU AND Be Gracious TO YOU.

Numbers 6:25

GRACE

PRAYER OF MOSES

MAY THE LORD SHOW YOU HIS FAVOR

FAVOR

FAVOR

FAVOR

FAVOR

Numbers 6:26

PRAYER OF MOSES

AND GIVE YOU HIS PEACE

PEACE

Numbers 6:26

Deuteronomy 28:2

Deuteronomy 28:2

MOSES' BLESSING

WHEREVER YOU GO, YOU WILL BE BLESSED

EVERYWHERE

EVERYWHERE

Deuteronomy 28:6

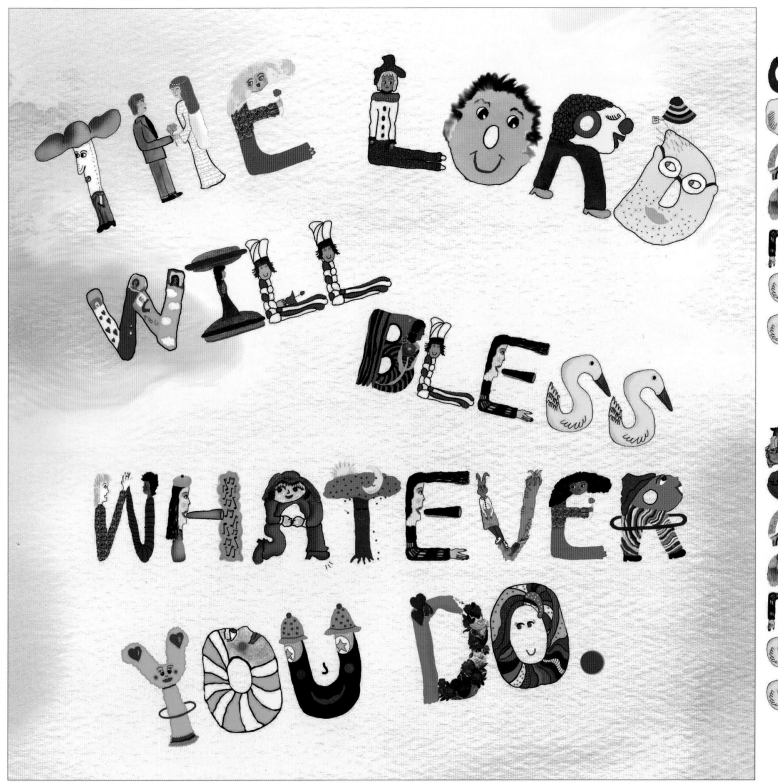

MOSES' BLESSING

THE LORD WILL BLESS WHATEVER YOU DO.

SUCCESS

Deuteronomy 28:8

MOSES' BLESSING

GOD'S PEOPLE

GOD'S PEOPLE

THE LORD WILL MAKE You HIS HOLY People

Deuteronomy 28:9

MOSES' BLESSING

OBEY OBEY

IF YOU WALK IN HIS WAYS.

OBEY OBEY

Deuteronomy 28:9

MOSES' BLESSING

RESPECT

RESPECT

THE LORD WILL MAKE YOU The Head And Not The Tail,

Deuteronomy 28:13

MOSES' BLESSING

AND YOU WILL RISE TO THE TOP.

RESPECT RESPECT

Deuteronomy 28:13

FRIEND OF GOD

FRIEND OF GOD

OH LORD, YOU HAVE SEARCHED MY HEART

Psalm 139:1

PRAYER OF DAVID

FRIEND OF GOD

AND YOU KNOW ALL ABOUT ME.

Psalm 139:1

PRAYER OF DAVID

FRIEND OF GOD

FRIEND OF GOD

YOU KNOW WHEN I SIT OR STAND.

Psalm 139:2

Psalm 139:2

Psalm 139:3

PRAYER OF DAVID

FRIEND OF GOD

AND YOU SEE ME WHEN I REST.

Psalm 139:3

Psalm 139:3

PRAYER OF DAVID

FRIEND OF GOD

FRIEND OF GOD

LORD, BEFORE I Speak, YOU KNOW WHAT I WILL SAY.

Psalm 139:4

Psalm 139:5

Psalm 139:5

PRAYER OF DAVID

The Angel Of The Lord Guards Those Who Respect Him, And He Delivers Them.

PROTECTION

Psalm 34:7

PRAYER OF DAVID

HAPPINESS

OH TASTE AND SEE THAT THE LORD IS GOOD:

HAPPINESS

Psalm 34:8

PRAYER OF DAVID

BLESSED IS THE MAN WHO TRUSTS IN HIM

Psalm 34:8

PRAYER OF DAVID

RESPECT THE LORD,
THOSE WHO
HONOR HIM
WILL HAVE
ALL
THEY NEED.

PROVISION

PROVISION

Psalm 34:9

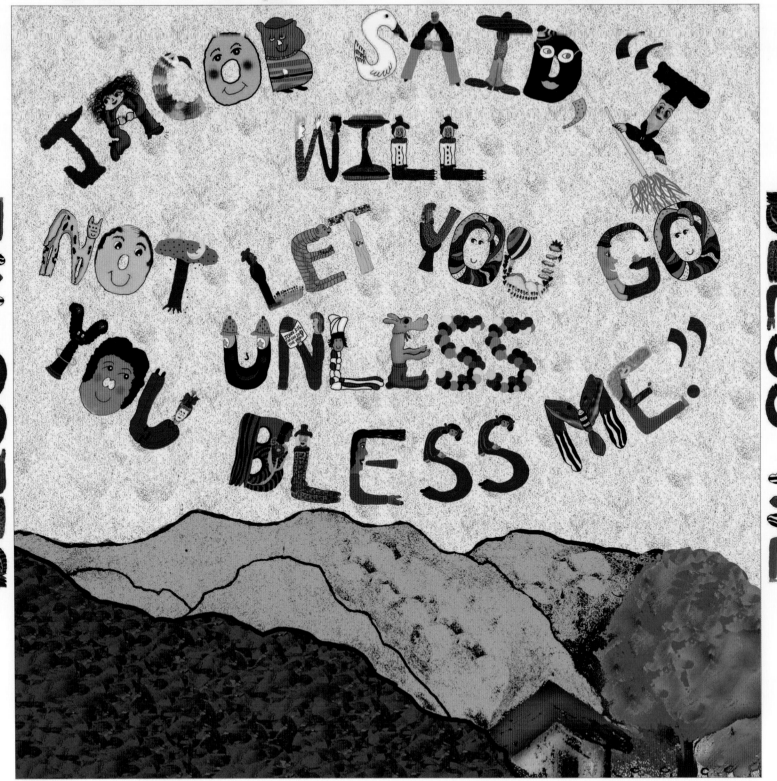

Genesis 32:26

JACOB'S PRAYER

AND GOD BLESSED HIM.

"BLESS ME"

"BLESS ME"

Genesis 32:29